I was really excited when I heard that Julia was writing another story for our lovely ladybird. I am so proud of *What the Ladybird Heard,* and it seems to be such a favourite with everyone. What a treat for me to be able to revisi___ ___rm and all our old friends, and a couple of new ones too! I was ple___ ___ hear that Hefty Hugh and Lanky Len are silly enough to take o___ ___le ladybird again. Some people never learn!

At the bac___ ___book you can see some of the drawings and paintings I did to ma___ ___ook. I always have to remember to put the ladybird on every p___ ___ ___ so small that I sometimes forget! Do look ou___ ___r. She gets into the strangest places! Have fun!

Lydia Monks

April 2015

Written by
Julia Donaldson

Illustrated by
Lydia Monks

What the Ladybird Heard NEXT

MACMILLAN CHILDREN'S BOOKS

Once upon a farm lived a ladybird,
And these are the things that she saw and heard:

The cow in her shed, the horse in his stall,
The cats who purred on the garden wall,
The barn full of straw, the field full of sheep,
The kennel where the dog lay fast asleep,
The fish in the pond, the drake and the duck,
The hive of bees and the heap of muck,
The hog in his sty, the goose in her pen,
And the coop which was home to the fat red hen.

Now the fat red hen with her thin brown legs
Laid lots and lots of speckled eggs
But then — oh help, oh no, oh dear —
Those eggs began to disappear.
Each morning all the eggs had gone.
And the animals asked, "What's going on?"

"I'll find out," said the ladybird.
So she flew and she flew, and she saw and she heard.

She saw two men in a big black van
With a torch and a sack and a cunning plan.
(They were Hefty Hugh and Lanky Len,
Who had been to jail but were out again.)
Said Lanky Len to Hefty Hugh, "Let's steal another egg or two."

But Hefty Hugh said, "Listen, Len:
I vote we steal the fat red hen.
We'll make our way to the chicken coop
And scoop her up in one fell swoop.
Just think of all those eggs she'll lay us,
And all the money folk will pay us!"

And Len replied, "We'll soon be rich.
It makes my fingers start to itch."

The little spotty ladybird
Told the animals what she'd heard:
"Hefty Hugh and Lanky Len
Are planning to steal the fat red hen!"

Then the cow said, "Moo!" and the hen said, "Cluck!"
"Hiss!" said the goose. "Quack!" said the duck.
"Neigh!" said the horse. "Oink!" said the hog,
"Baa!" said the sheep and "Woof!" said the dog,

And the two cats miaowed: "Those bad bad men!
We can't let them steal the fat red hen!"
But the ladybird said, "Listen, quick!
I've thought of a really clever trick."

At dead of night the two bad men
Opened the coop and snatched the hen.
But the fat red hen began to cluck,
"Why don't you steal the downy duck?

Her eggs are bigger far than mine
And people say they taste divine."

"Good thinking, that," said Lanky Len.
They tiptoed to the pond, but then . . .

The downy duck began to quack,
"Oh please don't put me in your sack.
Why don't you steal the goose instead?
She's bigger still, and better fed.
Her eggs are huge, and tasty too."
"Good thinking, that," said Hefty Hugh.

The duck joined in: "She's friendly, too.
I'm sure she'd love to live with you.
She'll put an end to all your cares.
You'll very soon be millionaires."
"Where is this Snerd?" asked Lanky Len.
"Not far away," chipped in the hen.
"She lives inside that big brown heap.
You'll find her there. She's fast asleep."

"What?" said Len, and "Who?" said Hugh.
The goose replied, "I thought you knew:
She lays the biggest eggs of all.
Each one looks like a rugby ball."

But when they tried to seize the goose
She hissed at them, "I'm not much use.
Why don't you steal that great big bird,
The super-duper Snuggly Snerd?"

The two thieves laughed: "We've got it made!
Let's take turns with the farmer's spade."
They dug and they dug, and Len said, "Pooh,
It stinks!" and Hugh said, "So do you."

And Len said, "Where's that giant bird,
The super-duper Snuggly Snerd?"
"She's rather shy," the goose replied.
"She must be hiding deep inside."

So they dug a tunnel, nice and deep.
"That's it!" said Hugh. "Now, in we creep."

"I think we're nearly there," said Len.
"The Snerd will soon be ours!" But then . . .

The heap collapsed, and Hugh said, "Yuk,
We're covered head-to-toe in muck."

And Len complained, "There *is* no Snerd.
They just made up that giant bird."

Then the other animals gathered round
And all let out a deafening sound.

NEIGH!

MOO!

OINK!

BAA!

WOOF WOOF!

MIAOW!

What a racket! What a row!

The farmer woke and said, "Goodness me!"
And he had a word with his prize Queen Bee,

And the bees chased after the two bad men,
Who never came back to the farm again!

Then the cow said, "Moo!" and the hen said, "Cluck!"
"Hiss!" said the goose. "Quack!" said the duck.
"Neigh!" said the horse. "Oink!" said the hog,
"Baa!" said the sheep and "Woof!" said the dog,
And the farmer cheered, and both cats purred,

But the ladybird said never a word . . .
And neither did the Snuggly Snerd.

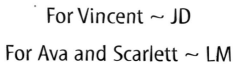

For Vincent ~ JD

For Ava and Scarlett ~ LM

First published 2015 by Macmillan Children's Books
an imprint of Pan Macmillan
a division of Macmillan Publishers International Ltd
Associated companies throughout the world
www.panmacmillan.com

ISBN: 978-1-4472-7595-4
Text copyright © Julia Donaldson 2015
Illustrations copyright © Lydia Monks 2015

1 3 5 7 9 8 6 4 2

A CIP catalogue record for this book is available from the British Library.

Printed in China

When I'm working on a new book, I read the story first. Then I like to start by drawing a rough plan of all the pages in the book. These are just tiny pencil sketches – sometimes called "thumbnails" because they are so small.

I also start to think about what the cover might look like.

Here are a couple of my early ideas for the cover.
See how much it has changed!

Next I start working on full-sized drawings, or "roughs", to work out the detail of the pictures.

These start out quite rough, then become cleaner and more finished when I am happy with how the picture is looking.

I also think about where the story text will go and leave space for it in the picture.